Timedetectors

MORNINGSIDE PRIMARY SCHOOL
Chatham Place
Hackney
London
E9 6LL
Tel: 0208 985 5382
Fax: 0208 986 6881
Headteacher: Jean Millham

Written by Darrel and Sally Odgers
Illustrated by Richard Hoit

To Ciff and Lavonne Stratton -
remembering the metal detector!

Written by Darrel & Sally Odgers
Illustrated by Richard Hoit

© 1995 Shortland Publications

09 08 07 06
12 11 10 9 8 7

Published in Australia and New Zealand by MIMOSA/McGraw-Hill
8 Yarra Street, Hawthorn, Victoria 3122
Published in the United Kingdom by Kingscourt/McGraw-Hill
Shoppenhangers Road, Maidenhead, Berkshire SL6 2QL

Printed in China through Bookbuilders

ISBN: 0-7901-0998-0

CONTENTS

Tasmania, located in the Southern Hemisphere, experiences the opposite season from the Northern Hemisphere. Summer in the Northern Hemisphere is June through to August, while summer in the Southern Hemisphere is December through to February. Therefore, the new school year in Tasmania begins just after the new calendar year.

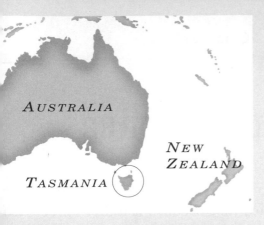

AUSTRALIA

NEW
ZEALAND

TASMANIA

TASMANIA

Asbestos Ranges • • Beaconsfield
• LAUNCESTON

• Franklin River
• Frenchman's Cap

• HOBART

NDIAN OCEAN

TASMAN SEA

Chapter 1

THE ADVENTURERS

I shouldn't have done it to Coxie. I mean, I wouldn't punch a dog in the face just because it didn't agree with me. So why did I have to go and punch Coxie? You can make up your mind when you've read what happened to Coxie and me.

Coxie and I are best friends. He's smaller than I am, and younger, and he wouldn't say boo to a goose. Plus, he's got this great big disadvantage he calls Mum. I don't mean she doesn't feed him and look after him. The thing is, she looks after him too well.

His mum hardly lets Coxie out of her sight without chasing after him with hats and coats and fifteen-plus sunscreen, and she's always fussing if he's home five minutes late. It's tough, but Coxie doesn't make much of a big deal of it. He puts up with it all, but I reckon he talks more to his cockatoo than to his mum. With a home life like that, who needs a punch in the chin from a so-called mate?

Coxie used to have a father and an elder brother who both died, so maybe that's what's wrong with his mum. She's lost two Coxes, so she wants to make sure of keeping the last of the line. And when I think of how close she came to losing him somewhere in the 32nd century, well...

Anyway, Coxie's OK. There's no harm in him, except he's too polite and believes the best of everyone. Now, Coxie and I belong to a group a bit like the scouts. It's called Adventurers, and it was started up by a couple of teachers from the local high school, where we go to school. These teachers – Mr Watts and Ms McCall – are a bit like Coxie. They reckon there's good in everyone, even high school kids.

They also reckon most kids need a kick in the pants to get them away from the telly and out adventuring. Great idea, Teach, but the thing is, kids can't adventure much in modern-day Tasmania. (That's where we live, Coxie and I, in Tasmania. It's an island south of the mainland of Australia, and it's also a state. It's got six cities and lots of towns, but there's plenty of room for rivers and bush and Tasmanian devils and other stuff, as well; at least, there's still plenty of room in the 1990s.)

It's OK for the adults. They can go bush-walking to Frenchman's Cap or whitewater rafting down the wild Franklin River whenever they want, but kids can't just head off on their own like that, because nobody lives near Frenchman's Cap or the wild Franklin. You've got to get there by car and that means conning someone into taking you.

Most kids can't take up flying or scuba-diving or hang-gliding or ballooning, either, because usually you need a licence to do these things or else it costs too much. So, Mr Watts and Ms McCall decided to start a club where we could have adventures without breaking our necks or our parents' bank accounts.

Coxie wanted to join Adventurers, no matter what. His mum said he'd hate it. Coxie said he'd love it. His mum said he'd get hurt. Coxie said he'd be careful. His mum said he'd catch pneumonia.

Coxie looked it up in the medical dictionary and pointed out that you don't "catch" pneumonia. His mum said she'd worry. Coxie nearly went into orbit. That's when my dad stuck his nose in.

"That poor kid," he said to my mum, "he doesn't get much of a break. Why don't you have a talk to Jan? She might not worry so much if she knew we were happy for Tom to join."

So Mum rang Coxie's mother.

"Well?" said Dad.

"She says he'll hate it," said Mum. "She says he went camping once. A huntsman spider fell on his face and he screamed all night."

"I'd scream if a huntsman spider fell on me," said Dad.

"Hey," I said, "Easter's coming up. Why don't we go camping and take Coxie with us? If he likes it, maybe Mrs Cox will stop fussing. If he hates it, maybe Coxie will stop fussing."

"You've got a brain or two in your head after all, Tom," said Dad, rubbing my hair. "Must have come from me."

"You're right," said Mum. "I've still got mine."

So that's what we did.

On Easter Monday, Mrs Cox sent Coxie over to our place with enough clothes for triplets and enough food for an army. Dad packed us up in the old station-wagon with two tents and some air mattresses, three sleeping-bags, a gas barbecue, and his new metal detector. Mum decided not to come. She said Dad's metal detector drove her mad.

"Always going beep and parp and yeeerp and getting me all excited over bottle caps," she said. "I'll paint the living-room instead." She started getting out drop sheets and paintbrushes straight off, so Dad got going. He's allergic to paint fumes, and so (of course) is Coxie.

We ribbed Dad about his metal detector for the first half-hour of the trip. It's so long its handle was stuck in the back seat and its snout (I mean the business end) was poking over between the two front seats. "Going to find gold, Dad?" I said. "Going to make us all millionaires?"

"Yeah, right. Joke's over," said Dad. He turned to Coxie. "Tom's always going on about my pet here, but I can guarantee that it does work."

"Yeah, on loose change you've buried in the sand," I said. "I bet you won't find a thing this trip, Dad."

"He might," said Coxie hopefully.

Dad rolled his eyes and I laughed. I might not have laughed so much if I'd known what that metal detector was going to detect on that trip, and how much trouble it was going to land me in. I mean, it was really the metal detector that led to me laying that punch on Coxie, and Coxie being kidnapped, and me being shot with a weapon like something out of *Star Trek*. I didn't enjoy it *that* much, I can tell you!

On the other hand, it also led to my meeting with Lizba Smith.

Chapter 2

ENVIRONMENTAL JAG

It took us about two hours to get to the Asbestos Ranges. There's a national park there, but you can't camp in it, so Dad took us along a side road outside the park. The Asbestos Ranges aren't very high as mountains go. I mean, if you're thinking about snow-capped peaks, frowning escarpments, and rare alpine plants, forget it. What they are is a series of tall, steep (very steep) hills running down to Bakers' Beach and nearly out to the old goldmine at Beaconsfield.

Most of the hills are covered in bush, but there are a few plantations of pine left on some of them. You reach the Ranges by driving along a rough road. It's like driving across a washboard, all bumpy and ridged. There are some signs but, if you don't know where you're heading, you're liable to end up going along a Forestry Commission road and getting lost. The soil (what there is of it) is pretty thin and a sort of yellowish, clayey stuff. The rocks stick out wherever there's been heavy rain, or where the trees are gone.

When we got to the Asbestos Ranges, we had to find a good place to camp. Dad drove along slowly, and told us to keep an eye out on both sides of the road. We needed a place that was flat and not too rocky. Dad wanted to be close to water for drinking and washing and stuff.

There are quite a few creeks running down out of the Ranges. Most of them are really deep and clear, because over the years, they've cut right down in the ground. The water tasted a bit earthy from the leaves and things, and Dad made us boil it before we drank any.

One of the creeks we found wasn't clear. The water was a soupy-looking brown.

"What's happened to that?" asked Coxie.

Dad stopped the wagon and got out. He took Coxie by the shoulders and turned him around. "See up there?" he said, pointing.

Coxie squinted. "That brown mark?"

"Yep. Cable-logging scar," said Dad. "It was done years ago. It's so steep here they used to drag the timber out with cables. Took all the undergrowth out with it, too. There isn't any depth of soil left, so the trees can't grow back. Every time it rains, what soil's left washes into the creek. That's why it's so brown."

"Yeah, yeah," I said. I didn't want Dad starting on his environmental jag. I mean, the timber mills employ a lot of people and I want a job when I leave school. Don't you? It would be good if we could have industry without doing any harm to the environment, but you can't have everything. Lizba knew that... but you don't know about Lizba yet. She comes into the story later on. She's dead now. It's odd to think of Lizba being dead. She had so much guts...

◆

We set up camp at the first clear creek beyond the cloudy one. Dad backed off the road into the cleared area near the creek and told Coxie and me to make a space for the tents. We picked up the bigger chunks of rock and a few dead branches, then Dad ran the rake over the site. There were big piles of pebbles here and there along the creek bank. Some of them were about half a metre across and as high as my knee. I didn't know what they were, so I tried to level one with the rake. Then I found out what they were, all right! They were jack-jumper nests! A lava flow of black soldier ants came boiling out, waving their pincers and looking for someone to bite.

Poor Coxie gave a bleat of fright. It scared me, too (those ants were big!), but I made out it didn't. "Cool it," I told Coxie. "They won't hurt if you keep clear of them."

"Especially if you don't poke their nests," said Dad. "Come on, Tom, make yourself useful." So I did.

It took us about an hour to get the camp set up. Dad told

us to keep our shoes and socks on. "You'll know it if you get one of those jack-jumpers up your leg," he said. "They're a lot worse than huntsman spiders."

"Lay off!" muttered Coxie. "I was only five years old when that spider fell on me, OK?"

Dad finished putting the tents up, and Coxie and I set up the larder. We had the butter and milk in plastic containers and we dunked them in the creek to keep them cool.

"Now listen," said Dad, when we'd finished. "You boys want to go off climbing the hills, right? Now that's OK, but you stick to that hill up there. Only go up this side, and make sure you come back down the side you go up. Watch out for snakes and spiders and jack-jumpers and other people, and stay together. Don't go off that hill except to come back to camp or along the creek. That way you can't get into much trouble."

We wouldn't have, but Dad never reckoned on the storm.

Chapter 3

UP THE CREEK

We had a great time that first day, and the second. I'm not going to tell you all the things we did. I've noticed that things that are great fun to do aren't often all that interesting to read about, so I'll skip ahead to the beginning of the exciting bit. We did climb the hill, of course, and we had to use our hands to pull ourselves up the steep bit, and Coxie got bitten by a jack-jumper that fell down his sleeve off a dead tree.

I twisted my ankle when I jumped off a fallen log into what looked like short grass, but turned out to be a whacking big hole full of longer grass.

We both ended up with scratches around the fronts of our legs from the prickly scrub.

We picked up lots of interesting bits of rock, and sticks with fungus on them, and Coxie found some tall, purplish pink flowers. "Mum'd really like these for her botany club," he said, "and those ferns by the creek."

While we were getting scratched and bitten and ankle-twisted, Dad was happily pottering up and down the stony creek bed with his metal detector. So, that was the first couple of days; Coxie and I were up and down the hills and Dad was paddling in the creek, cursing whenever he turned up a bottle cap. Yeah – there are bottle caps even in those nice, clear creeks. Criminal, isn't it?

The first night was OK; Coxie jumped and squeaked only three times. Once because he reckoned he could feel a jack-jumper crawling up his pyjama leg (he was right), and twice more because he reckoned the jack-jumper had fetched along his mates (he was wrong).

The second night, it rained. Or I should say, it poured. It teemed and soaked and thundered and lightninged and blew. At one point, I thought the tent was going to take off. I could hear the guy ropes thrumming in the wind, and the canvas was heaving like a cat in a bag. It was the worst storm I'd ever seen.

Once, Dad yelled out to ask us where we were.

"In the tent, of course!" I yelled back and burrowed down in my sleeping-bag. "Where else would we be?"

The storm was over by morning, but Dad had been awake half the night worrying about the tents falling down, so he said he'd have a kip now. "Watch what you do this morning," he said. "There could be trees down, and it'll be greasy underfoot. Oh, and keep your eye out for strangers. I thought I saw someone prowling around last night."

Coxie and I had breakfast, then hung out our sleeping-bags to air. It was too slippery to climb the hills, so we poked about the creek for a bit. After that, we decided to check out some of the other creeks.

The first one we came to was the one that was all brown from the run-off that came down the hills from the cable-logging scar. Because of the silt in the water, this creek had spongy banks, held together by soggy grass and matted roots.

We waded upstream a bit. It was cold, but we were having the time of our lives, leeches and all. I suppose we pushed upstream a couple of hundred metres. The creek got deeper, and in one place disappeared underground. We could hear it gurgling along under the spongy ground, so we went a bit further, and that's where we found the collapsed bank.

It was part of what you might call the "roof" of the underground creek, and this big lump of soil and leaf-mould and rock had fallen in, making a murky pool. A big shoulder of rock stuck out, grey basalt, with fat seams of white quartz. The quartz had brownish yellow streaks in it.

"Wow!" said Coxie. "Reckon that's gold, Tom?"

"Nah," I said. "Couldn't be so lucky. The place has been mined out, I reckon."

"This rock's been under the ground until now," pointed out Coxie. "Let's get your dad."

I know Dad's always like a bear with a sore head if you wake him up, so I made another suggestion. "Let's get the metal detector! We can run tests, so we'll know if it's worthwhile."

I knew I wasn't supposed to use Dad's detector without him. I wouldn't have if I'd been on my own, but I knew Dad wouldn't yell at me in front of Coxie, so I thought I was safe. All the same, I moved quietly. The detector was lying beside Dad's tent. It doesn't weigh much, but it's like a fishing-rod or a weed-eater – you have to be careful how you carry it. Coxie wanted to carry it, but I said I'd look after the detector. It would be my hide nailed to the wall if anything broke.

It was a bit of a scramble getting it to the right place, and then I had to remember how Dad had shown me how to tune it to the ground. When you see people using metal detectors on telly, they just stick the snout of the thing down on the ground, it goes "Peeerp!" – and bingo! They've hit gold! I can tell you it isn't that simple. I strapped the Velcro band across my arm, put on the earphones, and started to tune the detector to the ground. Sand registers differently from grass, and watery banks register differently from dry rock.

It took me about ten minutes just to get the thing tuned, and by then my arm was aching so much I had to rest. Then I started detecting in the wide puddle that the creek was making.

I couldn't see the bottom because of the dirt, so I stumbled a few times. Coxie kept leaping about on the bank and saying, "Try the rock, Tom, try the rock!"

"In a minute," I said. "I've got to get the feel of the place first."

Really, I think I was just putting it off, because I knew it couldn't really be gold. Kids like me just don't find gold. Kids like me find bottle caps and rusting beer cans...

◆

Finally, to stop Coxie nagging, I did run the detector over the rock. And I was right – it wasn't gold. There's a red needle that swings around on the dial, pivoting between gold, tin, silver, iron, and hot rock. It must have been iron oxide or something, I think, because it was low down on the dial. I was ready to stop, but Coxie started ripping up the matted roots that hung out over the lip of the bank.

"Cut it out," I said. "You're souping it up even more!"

"There's something hard under here," said Coxie; so, just to shut him up, I passed the detector's snout over the torn-up roots and the hard lump underneath.

The detector went wild.

Chapter 4

THE SKULL

"It's gold!" yelled Coxie.

"Shut up!" I said. If it was gold, I didn't want the wo
to know. OK, so Coxie and Dad and I were probably
only people around, but Dad had thought he'd s
someone the night before – and the sort of people v
dump beer cans and junk in creeks might do anything.

I laid aside the detector (carefully) and helped Co
drag the stuff out of the roots. It was difficult work,
our fingertips were pretty sore by the time we rolled
lump up onto the solid ground.

It was about as big as a basketball, knobby, and cove
in mud and roots. It was heavy enough to be awkward,
not as heavy as it should have been for its size if it had b
pure rock.

It wasn't gold, because gold is heavier than most ro
not lighter. Anyway, when we washed it off, it was grey
white, with bits of brown stuck here and there like rais
in Mum's fruit cake. There was one chunk of whitish s
that looked like bone...

"It's a hunk of conglomerate," I said.

"Pudding stone, Mum calls it," said Coxie. "It's all so
of different sorts of stone mixed together. You sometir
get lumps of it along the river. It's pretty light, thou
isn't it?"

"Maybe it's hollow," I said. I checked it out with
detector again, and the detector went crazy. The tone

registering solid metal, but the needle wanted to go anticlockwise and pinned itself hard to the left-hand side of the dial. The plate of the detector seemed to be trying to stick to the ball of rock, as if it were magnetic. Weird, because the plate was made of plastic.

"It thinks there's something in there," said Coxie. "Let's break it open."

I picked up a lump of basalt.

"No!" yelled Coxie. "Use a hammer!" But I'd already dropped the rock. The pudding stone broke with a sort of popping sound. There was this foul smell.

"Ugh!" spluttered Coxie, and grabbed for his inhaler. (Did I tell you Coxie is asthmatic? Well, he is.) "What's that?"

The smell was gone in a moment. The pudding stone had cracked open like a coconut shell, and the bit of bone stuck right out. It really was bone all right, but it wasn't the right colour. It had gone all blue and green and pearly.

"It's opalized!" said Coxie. "Look." He picked it up and started prying it out of the pudding stone. It was a human skull.

Coxie dropped it and stepped back. I don't blame him. I don't know if you've ever held a skull in your hands, but there's nothing quite like its empty stare. It gives you the shivers.

"It's plaster," said Coxie. "It's a fake."

"Come on," I said. "It's been wrapped up in a hunk of rock!"

"So someone put it there," said Coxie. "Like they put Piltdown Man in the ground. Like they put that limestone statue in the ground and P. T. Barnum dug it up and said it was a prehistoric giant. Like they put..."

"Listen," I said. "What are you afraid of? It's a real skull, but no one can blame you for it. Bone doesn't opalize overnight, and even if it's been here only five or six years you're not likely to have been out murdering people when you were seven." All the same, I was uncomfortable, too. The eye sockets were looking at me from the ground.

Apart from that, it wasn't so bad. It wasn't brown and broken like most skulls you see on TV, and it didn't have any mummified skin or hair hanging from it. It was just a clean pearly, greenish blue skull. It was beautiful, I guess, if you thought of it as an ornament, instead of part of a dead person. I could imagine Mum cooing over it and setting it in her display cabinet at home.

"There's something else here," said Coxie after a minute. He was feeling around in the broken bits of pudding stone and he pulled out a chain with a medallion on the end. It was quite big, about the size of the palm of my hand, and it was a funny colour, like a silver teapot that's been very hot, if you can imagine that.

"This must have been what that detector was picking up," said Coxie, swinging the medallion. "Think it's silver, Tom?"

"Put it down and I'll check," I said. I ran the detector over it and again the dial went wild. It didn't seem to think the medallion was silver or gold or iron or tin or even hot rock. "It's gone wrong," I said. "Dad'll have my guts for garters!"

"Let's try it on something else," said Coxie.

I was wearing a gold-plated earring, so Coxie held the snout of the detector up against my head. It didn't want to work at all, so he dropped some loose change on the ground. I ran the detector over that.

It seemed to register normally. "That means it's working OK," I said. "Phew! What a relief! I thought the thing had gone wild. Let's turn it off before something really *does* happen to it."

I tested the medallion again, with the same result as

20

before – a good, strong tone. I switched it off. The dial went slack, but the tone kept right on registering. "It's busted!" I yelled. "It's gone wrong. Dad's going to murder me!"

"No, look," said Coxie. He squinted at the medallion. "What I think is..."

I didn't find out what Coxie thought because I heard Dad yelling.

"Thom – as! Cox – ie!"

"O-Oh," I said. "He doesn't sound too happy. He'll probably kill me twice over... We'd better get out of here."

I grabbed the detector from Coxie. "Get the skull!"

Coxie looked as if he thought it might bite, but then he picked up the opalized skull and wrapped it in his shirt. He dropped the medallion into his pocket and we took off.

Dad was really mad when we got back to camp. For a start, he was riled because we'd disappeared. Then, he was riled because we hadn't answered him. Then he was really, really riled that we'd taken the metal detector.

I'd been wrong about him not tearing a strip off me in front of Coxie – he let me have both barrels and then some. He snatched up the detector and tested it over and over, but it seemed to be working OK by then.

Phew! I thought. I'll get murdered only once over, after all!

I'm not telling you all this so you'll feel sorry for me – I'm telling you so you'll see why we showed him the skull. We wanted to take his mind off us.

It took his mind off us, all right, but we soon wished we hadn't shown him, because he insisted on taking the skull straight to the police. And that ended that camping trip.

It might have ended the whole thing, but it didn't. Coxie still had the medallion in his pocket.

Chapter 5

CARBON 14

That was the last Coxie and I saw of the opalized skull. The police (who aren't the idiots some TV shows make out) didn't jump to the conclusion that I'd murdered the owner of the skull. They didn't arrest Coxie or Dad, either.

Oh, they were a bit stern at first. They thought it was a fake and a hoax, especially when Dad said Coxie and I had found it. Then Dad asked how we could possibly have faked an opalized skull out there in the Asbestos Ranges.

"They're only kids, you know. And they've got a lot of better things to do with their time than stay up nights making an elaborate skull. They would need a great deal more technical expertise and money than either of them have access to," he explained. "If it isn't real, it's a work of art."

So then the police decided that we'd been hoaxed by someone else. Anyway, they agreed that even if it was real, it couldn't possibly belong to any modern murder victim. They thanked Dad for reporting the matter and said they'd look into it, and that was that.

"Don't we get it back?" I asked. (I wanted to give it to Mum for her cabinet.)

Dad shrugged. He was a bit miffed at the lack of interest. "I don't know," he said. "I doubt it. I think state legislation says the public can't own bones – unless they came out of the Sunday roast, of course."

"I thought anything you metal-detected was yours," I said.

"It is – within reason," said Dad. "Unless it's something

valuable like a gold chain with the owner's name engraved on the clasp. In that case, I'm obligated to notify the owner – or the police."

"You did that, and the police kept it," I said.

"A skull's a bit different from a gold chain," said Dad. "It can hardly be returned to the owner, but I expect they'll try to find out whose it was. How did you come to find it, anyway? It isn't metallic."

"No," I said, "but –" I was about to tell Dad about the medallion (which I'd actually forgotten about, can you believe it?) when Coxie interrupted.

"Maybe it had gold fillings in its teeth," said Coxie.

Dad looked at him sideways. "Ha. Ha."

◆

When we got home, Mum was surprised to see us. "Rained out?" she suggested.

"No," said Dad, "we found a skull."

"Oh." Mum looked thoughtful. "Whose?"

While Dad explained, I hauled Coxie off to my room. "OK, let's see that necklace thing."

Coxie locked the door and showed me the medallion.

"We ought to have handed that over, too," I said.

"I sort of forgot I had it," said Coxie.

"If it's got a name on it, we'll have to hand it in," I said.

Coxie turned the disc over. "No name." He swung it back and forth on its chain. It wasn't particularly beautiful or anything, but still I found my eyes following. "Hey, cut it out!" I said. "What are you trying to do – hypnotize me?"

"Could be," said Coxie, but he stopped swinging the medallion. "So what do we do? Hand it over, or what?"

I took it from him. If we hadn't gone metal-detecting in the creek, no one would have it. Since we had, why shouldn't we keep it?

"Let's wait until the police get back to us," I said. "If they ask if we found anything else, we'll hand it over. Otherwise, we'll hang on to it. It isn't as if it's valuable or anything..."

"No," agreed Coxie. Of course, we were wrong about that. "It can't do any harm," said Coxie.

He was wrong about that, too, but how were we supposed to know?

◆

Coxie's mum came over to collect him. She was so glad to see him in one piece that she gave in and said OK, then, he could join the Adventurers. So we did. It was fun, but nothing else important happened until a few weeks later, when Dad called the police to see if they'd gotten anywhere.

I think they'd practically forgotten the skull, because he got passed through several people and put on hold; then he was told someone would get back to him.

"Red tape!" said Dad between his teeth. "No wonder the country's going down the drain."

But a week or so later, someone did get back to him.

"Well, Tom, your skull's a bit of a mystery," said Dad.

I grabbed my head with both hands and made woo-woo-woo! noises. Dad cuffed me jokingly. "The skull you found, boy. Not *your* skull. They say it seems to be genuine opalized bone. The only thing is..."

"What?" said Mum.

Dad laughed. "They figure it's far too old to have been where you boys found it."

"That's a bit of a contradiction, isn't it?" said Mum. "It was probably some poor old prospector from last century."

"It's a good bit older than that, apparently," said Dad.

"An Aborigine, perhaps?"

"Hmm," said Dad. He rubbed his nose. "That's the

obvious conclusion, but they say this skull isn't Aboriginal. The contours are all wrong."

"A shipwrecked sailor?" said Mum. "A Viking, maybe."

"She," said Dad. "That's one thing they do know. It's the skull of a woman, about forty-five years old."

"A shipwrecked sailor's wife?" suggested Mum. "A Vikingess?"

"Who knows?" said Dad. "In any case, they've sent the thing to be carbon dated. That should shed some more light on the subject."

I don't know if you've ever heard of carbon dating, but as far as I can work out, it's like this: scientists take some material and measure something called carbon 14, which is its radioactivity, to get an idea of its age. They can't do it with stone or water or metal, because the stuff has to have been alive. Wooden ships can be carbon dated, but iron ones can't. Cotton, wool, and linen cloth can, but nylon can't. Amber can, because it used to be sap before it got fossilized, but diamonds can't. Paper can, because it's made from wood. And so can bone. It's a bit like the stuff you can and can't add to a compost pile.

What happens is that the radioactivity starts to decay as soon as living stuff stops living. After a time – thousands of years – half the radioactivity has gone. That leaves half what there was in the first place.

After the same time again, half the half that was left has gone. That leaves a quarter.

After the same time again, half the quarter is gone, and that leaves an eighth. The new techniques actually count the number of carbon 14 atoms left in the material, but it's all pretty technical.

"How accurate is it?" I asked Dad.

"Oh, very," said Dad. "Up to plus or minus a few hundred years."

Plus or minus a few hundred years? I thought Dad was being sarcastic, but I looked it up in a few books and found he was right. When you're talking thousands of years, an estimate of plus or minus a few hundred is quite accurate.

The results of the carbon dating came back a few months later. By then, Christmas had come and gone and we'd started a new year at school. I'd sort of half-forgotten about the skull, so it took me by surprise when Dad told me my girlfriend was a very old lady indeed.

"Eh?" I said. "I haven't got a girlfriend."

"That skull you and Coxie unearthed last Easter," said Mum helpfully.

"Oh yes," I said. "So how old is it?"

Dad frowned. "The report said it was more than 5,000 years old," he said, "but they knew that couldn't be possible, so they ran the tests again. Then they tried with potassium-argon dating, which is what they use for older fossils, but that didn't work out. They came up with a round figure of 5,500 years. And that's got to be wrong."

"Why?" I asked.

Dad buried his face in his hands. "Does this boy know nothing?" he asked. "Look, Tom, the skull is European."

"Great," I said. "So what?"

"So," said Dad slowly, "if this skull is as old as they say, it can't have been where you found it. Europeans didn't reach Australia until a few hundred years ago."

"So they're wrong, and she was an Aborigine," I said.

"No, she isn't," said Dad. And he was right. She wasn't.

Chapter 6

PILTDOWN LADY

When scientists come up with an answer that can't be right, they juggle the facts around until they come up with something better.

It might not please them at all, but it pleases them a lot more than admitting that everything they've always believed has got to be wrong. So the scientists who ran the tests on the skull decided this: The skull was over 5,000 years old, was European, and had been found in a Tasmanian creek.

But: The skull couldn't be 5,000 years old, European, and found in a Tasmanian creek. Not unless it had been put there in the past 400 years.

Therefore: **(a)** the skull must be younger than it seems (like 4,600 years younger) **(b)** the skull couldn't be European **(c)** the skull couldn't have been found in a Tasmanian creek.

They decided (c) was the way to go, but though they poked back into local history, they couldn't trace any missing prehistoric skulls that Coxie and I could have stolen and planted in that creek. So they went to work on (b). The only trouble was that however often they looked at the skull, it still wasn't Aboriginal. In the end, they came to the only theory that seemed to fit the facts.

The skull must be a very old, very well-preserved European-type skull that had been placed in a Tasmanian creek by a person or persons unknown, and then dug out of that same creek between one and four hundred years later by Coxie and me.

I can see why they didn't come up with the truth, because that was unbelievable.

The newspapers ran stories on the skull, but most of them took the line that it was all a hoax. At the newspaper stands, you could read the headlines across the stacks. One headline said, **"PILTDOWN LADY?"** and another one said, **"PULL THE OTHER ONE, PROF!"**

The Aboriginal community called for an independent check to be made to make quite certain it wasn't Aboriginal, and then everyone lost interest.

"Well?" I said to Dad. "Do we get it back? I want to put it in the cabinet."

"No," said Dad. "That seems to be the only thing everyone agrees on. Nobody's claiming your lady as a relative or even a distant acquaintance, there's not a hope of identifying her, and there's no way of sending her home. She could be Russian or British or Norse or German or... well, she could be almost anything from the European continent."

"Or Martian," I said.

"Told you," said Mum smugly. "She's a Viking lady."

"Quite probably," said Dad, "but we don't get her back. I expect she'll end up in the lower left-hand drawer in a filing cabinet somewhere."

And maybe she did.

Dad and Mum were wrong about her being a Viking lady, though. Lizba was (is? will be?) as Australian as I am... but Coxie and I are the only ones who know that.

I must say I was annoyed at the way things went. I'd wanted to keep the skull, and I wouldn't have minded some publicity, either. I mean, when those two kids found an antique egg a few years back in Western Australia, they were interviewed on TV and everything. It seemed hard that just because our find was human, there wouldn't be anything in it for us.

"Just as well you didn't hand over that medallion," I said to Coxie. "The police would have put *that* in a filing cabinet, too. Where is it, anyway?"

Coxie dipped his hand down the front of his shirt and hauled up the medallion by its chain. It looked a lot better than when I'd last seen it. "I polished it," explained Coxie.

"Gee." It did look good. "Hey," I said, "it's my turn to keep it, isn't it?"

Coxie opened his mouth a time or two, like a cod. "I found it," he pointed out.

"With our metal detector," I reminded him.

"It was my idea to use it," Coxie persisted.

"If it hadn't been for me," I said, "you wouldn't have been in the Ranges at all. If you hadn't been in the Ranges, you wouldn't have had a chance to use the metal detector, and if you hadn't..."

"OK, OK!" said Coxie. "Here. You wear it for a while, but don't let your mum or dad see it. They'll probably want to take it to the police."

◆

Dad's got a whole big shelf of books about the past (Dad's got books about everything!), so that night I looked through them for anything like the medallion. I got a bit sidetracked with gruesome pictures of Egyptian mummies and people who were buried by the eruption of Mt. Vesuvius at Pompeii, but I did find photos of jewellery and coins.

A heap of gold jewellery had come out of Egyptian King Tutankhamen's tomb, and there was an arm bracelet that had belonged to someone called Cyrus the Great – but none of it looked like the medallion. The nearest were silver coins, but the medallion was easily twice as big and twice as thick as any of them. I couldn't ask anyone about it in case it ended up in a cop shop filing cabinet.

"Oh, what the heck?" I said to my dog. "I suppose it's plastic or something. I suppose the whole thing was a joke."

But who could have played the joke, and why? Who would bury a skull and a medallion in the Asbestos Ranges? There would be no guarantee that anyone would find it, ever. Unless Dad had done it... But no. Dad might have played a joke on Coxie and me, but he'd never have dragged the police into it.

I gave up on books and looked closely at the medallion. I don't think I've described it properly yet. Well, it was a sort of burned silver colour, and the size of the palm of my hand. One side was flat and smooth; the other side had a sort of braille clockface. There were tiny little slits around the edge, a bit like the ridges on the edge of a coin.

That makes it sound just like any old locket or medallion – but there was more. See, it wasn't only the metal detector that acted strangely when the medallion was around. It upset other electronic devices, too. Coxie had had quite a run-in with Mr Watts over that at school; every time Coxie went near the computer to have his turn, the computer started yelling for help. Well, practically.

Now, I spent a while teasing the clock radio by swinging the medallion back and forth in front of it. The radio part was turned off, but whenever the medallion swung past, there'd be this burst of static.

After a while, I started running my fingernails around the grooves, trying to set my teeth on edge. One of my nails was a bit longer than the others (I hadn't gotten around to biting it yet), and it went right to the depth of the slits. Then it caught on a ridge, and the medallion lit up. Suddenly, I could see the numbers around the disc as plain as day! The numbers ran towards the centre in a sort of spiral pattern. I jerked my fingernail out, and the numbers faded to silver again. I tried it a few more times, and it did the same each time. Nothing else happened, so after a while, I put the medallion away in my pocket.

Chapter 7

BACK TO THE RANGES

By the time Easter came again, Coxie and I had been members of Adventurers for a year. We'd been rappelling and water-skiing and camping with the club, and now it was our turn to have a Lone Adventure. In Lone Adventures, we get to do things on our own – or with a friend. We have to organize it ourselves, decide what to take and everything.

Of course, we're only alone up to a point. Mr Watts can't dump us in the Ranges and leave. What if a bushfire started? We'd get barbecued, and he'd get sued. No, the way it works is this: the adventurers set up camp in one place and a leader sets up a few hundred metres away. He (or she, if it's Ms McCall) minds his own business and pretends not to be there unless there's an emergency, or an adventurer asks for help.

Coxie and I gathered our stuff, and Mr Watts took us to the Ranges. "Where do you boys want to be dropped off?" he asked. "Anywhere in mind?"

We directed Mr Watts to the place we'd camped with Dad. Mr Watts looked at us a bit suspiciously – of course, he knew about the skull, but it's part of the rules of the club that he can't give advice unless we ask, so he dropped us off with our gear. He handed Coxie a UHF CB radio for emergencies. The radio crackled wildly with static.

"Don't tell me it's on the blink," said Mr Watts.

Coxie gave it to me, and it settled down. "It's OK now, Mr

Watts," I said. "I reckon Coxie's got too much static electricity in his body. You've seen what he does to the computer!"

"Pull the other one, Tom!" said Mr Watts. He gave us a grin and drove off.

We knew he'd be only around the corner, but it felt weird when he'd disappeared. Unless something really bad happened, we were on our own.

It was warm for April, and Coxie took off his shirt. I could see the medallion shining in the sun. He probably thought he looked like an Aztec warrior or something, but what he really looked like was a skinny eleven-year-old kid wearing his sister's necklace. We pitched the tent and got everything ready, and then we looked at one another.

"Well – let's go," I said, and we went back to the muddy creek.

I don't think we expected to find anything else there, and it didn't seem likely we would, because we couldn't find the right place. Oh, we found the creek all right, but the part that had been underground the year before had caved in, and it had been dug over like a vegetable garden.

I kicked at the mud. We should have known everyone would have been snooping around up here. After all, it had been a year. Why hadn't I nagged Dad to bring me back?

"I wish we hadn't shown the skull to Dad," I said. "We might as well have kept it, don't you think? Seeing what's happened to it now."

I squinted up the hill. The cable-logging scar was as brown and raw-looking as before, and the creek was as muddy. "Let's climb up," I said.

It was a real scramble up that hill. Actually, it was two hills, with a flat top and a little fold between. We had a rest in the fold, then went on, sweating and gasping. Coxie's shoulders were all covered with pieces of dead leaves and flakes of dirt. You could see where the run-off had been pouring all winter, even down where the trees still were. There were dirty tracks where flows of mud had come down the hill before running into the creek at the bottom.

Coxie was climbing in the dried mud track, because it was easier underfoot than the prickly bush grass and undergrowth. The medallion kept flipping against his chest as he climbed, so he took it off. He was about to put it in his pocket when he stopped short and sat down hard in the mud, staring at the medallion in his hand.

"What's up?" I said. "Another jack-jumper? They really seem to..."

Coxie shoved the medallion into my hand, as if he were playing "Hot Potato". The sun glinted off the metal, and the numbers were glowing. Not only glowing, but shifting around like the images in a hologram or a three-dimensional picture. It gave me the creeps, and I almost dropped the medallion. All those shifting numbers made me feel weird, especially since they seemed to be shifting backwards or anticlockwise.

"What is it?" asked Coxie. "Has it gone radioactive or something?"

"Let's hope not," I said, "or we're history." I put the medallion on a piece of bark, and Coxie and I backed off and hid behind a fallen log. I'm no chicken, but what's the sense in sitting still when a bomb could go off in your face?

We lay there, sweating. When the suspense got to be too much, I poked my nose over the log.

"What's it doing?" asked Coxie.

"Still the same. It reminds me of something."

"Yeah, a killer croc waiting to take your leg off," muttered Coxie.

"No..." I clicked my fingers. "You know that video game arcade in town? The medallion's making the same pattern over and over, like the games do before you put your money in."

"Well, I'm not about to stick any money in it," said Coxie.

We couldn't stay behind the log forever, so we edged back towards the medallion, which was still shifting backwards through its numbers. I dabbed my finger on it quickly, in case it burned me. It was cool, so I picked it up. I walked a few steps uphill, and the flickering got worse. It built up until I could hardly stand to look at the thing; then, as I kept climbing, it started to fade away. I went back to Coxie.

The medallion got brighter.

I'm not thick, and I doubt if you are, either. The thing was playing hot and cold with us.

"I wonder what it's homing in on?" said Coxie. "I don't like this."

We trudged up and down and around and around, taking turns carrying the medallion.

"Hot... cold... warm," we kept muttering, as the flickering got brighter or dimmer. Then suddenly, it was "boiling".

The place didn't look promising. It was slap bang in the middle of the run-off track, and the ground was stuck full of nasty, sharp edges of rock sticking up through the dry mud. Still, I took out my hunting knife (actually, it's Dad's hunting knife I'd borrowed for camping) and started scratching at the ground.

The mud flaked up easily, and soon I was prying little rocks out with the knife point. "I hope whatever it is isn't too deep," I said. "The ground's like solid rock under here." I pried up a round rock and pulled at a long tendril of root. "These roots are really tough," I said. "It's grown right through an old bandicoot bone."

Coxie bent over and started working it out of the ground. As he worked, the sun beat down on his back. I warned

him to put on his shirt before he turned into a lobster.

When he finally pulled the tendril free, I saw it wasn't a root, after all, but the chain of another medallion, tangled around a splinter of bone. Coxie dripped some water out of the flask over the medallion, and as soon as it was clean, we could see it was flashing and flickering, just like the one we already had.

So there we were. Two medallions, both flickering and shifting their numbers about, and a few splinters of rotten old bone. And I mean rotten, because they snapped between my fingers like old twigs. "D'you reckon this is some more of the same person?" I asked.

I suppose it sounds pretty gruesome, me sitting there, breaking up human bones with my fingers, but that's what I did do, and it's important. If I hadn't been busy messing about with those splinters, it might have been me who started the medallions working. But it wasn't. It was Coxie.

Chapter 8

TIMESTORM

So, one minute I was squatting in the dry mud, snapping bones like toothpicks in the April sunlight; the next, Coxie was saying, "Hey, this one's going clockwise... I wonder if the grooves fit together?"

I heard him fiddling with the two medallions, pushing them face to face. There was a click as they engaged, then...

Everything was black, except for some really impressive streaks of lightning – then, what felt like a whole bath-tub full of water came crashing down over my shoulders. It was like stepping out of a warm, well-lit house into a really fiendishly thunder-storming blackness. No, it was worse, because when you step out of a house into a storm, you already know the storm's going on, so you know what to expect. I know I gasped. I think I let out a yell, too. OK then, it was more like a scream. Coxie screamed, too, actually – anyone would have.

"What is it?" I gasped. "An eclipse, or what?"

Really, I knew eclipses come on slowly, but what would you have thought if you'd been plunged from sunny daylight into stormy darkness in less than a second?

"Maybe we've been bombed," said Coxie. His voice was shaking. I remember thinking if he was right, we'd probably be dead soon, and that Coxie wouldn't be such a bad person to die with. I wouldn't ever choose to die alone. Lizba died alone, but that was her choice and, as I said, she doesn't come into the story just yet.

Bombs or no bombs, we were already drenched and frozen. I heard Coxie cough two or three times and start to wheeze, and I knew he was going into one of his asthma attacks. "Get your puffer out, you idiot!" I yelled at him. "What are you doing?"

"Here." Coxie shoved the medallions at me and dug in his day pack for the inhaler.

I shoved the medallions in my pockets, one in each, and then – the storm stopped. It was daylight again and the sun was shining.

The only sounds I could hear, apart from Coxie's gasps and my own noisy breathing, were a stutter from the CB and the soft swish of wind in the gum-trees.

"Wow!" I said, when I'd got my breath back. "Far out!"

Coxie shivered. He had his wheezing just about under control, but he looked pinched and a bit blue.

"That was as bad as the storm we had here last year," I said. I was still feeling shaky, but one of us had to say something. "Remember? When the tents nearly blew away?"

Coxie's teeth were chattering so much, he sounded like a tap-dancer on TV. "L-l-l... g-g-g," he said.

"I suppose we'd better go back and dry off," I said. "And call Mr Watts to let him know we're OK."

I had the CB slung over my shoulder, and it was stuttering like crazy. The medallions were interfering, and when I tried to call, I couldn't get through. "Here, take them," I said. "They're making it go berserk." I pulled the medallions out and swung them at Coxie. He backed off so quickly that he fell over a log and sat down hard on the other side. Then he grabbed my arm and nearly dragged me down as well.

"Cut it out, Coxie!" I said. "The storm's over, and we didn't drown."

"The ground's dry," gasped Coxie.

It was. I picked up a bit of bark and held it up to the light. Not a shadow of damp, not a bead of water. Suddenly, I was shaking as hard as Coxie. "We dreamed it," I said. "It was a hal– a what-do-you-call-it?"

"Hallucination," said Coxie. "It wasn't." He wrung out a dribble of water from his shirt. "Hallucinations can't make you wet," said Coxie.

He was right. Out in the bush, it's rain that makes you wet. The thing is, rain makes the ground wet, too. After the downpour we'd just had, the trees should have been dripping, but they were dry. The air was dry.

Since Coxie wouldn't take them, I dropped the medallions and backed off until the CB stopped crackling. Then I called Mr Watts.

"Anything wrong, Tom?" He sounded surprised.

"Thought you might be worried about us, that's all."

"Now why would I worry about a healthy pair like you and Coxie?"

"You might if there was an eclipse," I said. "You might if there was a thunder and lightning downpour."

"I might if there was an earthquake, too," said Mr Watts, in a dry sort of voice. "Since there isn't, I'm not worried. Where are you?"

"Halfway up the hill," I said.

"Watch out for snakes," said Mr Watts, and signed off.

Coxie and I stood staring at one another and dripping onto the dry ground.

"Could have been a local storm," I said.

"So local it didn't wet the ground." Coxie put away his puffer. His hands were shaking. "So local it stopped raining before it hit the ground."

I took a deep breath. "So – what did you do?" I asked. "What did you do with those medallions?"

Coxie shrugged. "I just sort of twisted them together so the grooves meshed."

"And they made a thunderstorm," I said.

Coxie frowned. "Remember you said it was like the one we had when we were here last year?"

"Yeah," I said. "But that was at night, and it did wet the ground."

"It was night here for a few seconds."

"What are you getting at?" I asked.

"Maybe it was the same storm!"

"But that would mean we'd gone back in time," I said, "and here we are. I just talked to Mr Watts."

"I bet you couldn't have talked to Mr Watts while the storm was going on. He wasn't here that night."

I could see what he was getting at, but it seemed crazy. "You're mad," I said.

"Yeah."

"I suppose we could run another test," I said. "If we go back down to the camp and try it again."

We didn't talk as we climbed down the hill. Our shirts dried quickly, but my shorts were still damp when we got to the camp. "OK," I said. "Do whatever you did before."

We moved to the edge of the camp-site, picking our way around jack-jumper nests. "OK," I said, handing him the medallions, "make them do it again."

I didn't think it would work. If I had, I probably wouldn't have had the guts to do it. All the same, it was a stupid thing to do. Dad's always saying not to mess around with things I don't understand, and if these medallions really had caused a timestorm, we were risking more than the mild electric shock or bright blue fingers I'd gotten when I'd messed around with things before.

Coxie put the medallions together, face to face. His hands were shaking like crazy. "The grooves lock into one

41

another," he said. "Sort of like cogs in a wheel. I just gave them a twist like this..."

I think he twisted his right hand clockwise and his left hand anticlockwise. I didn't really see, because we were in the wet dark again. Thunder, lightning, pouring rain. I peered around in the next flash, and there was the camp... or was it? Something was wrong.

"What's different?" I yelled at Coxie.

There was a really big flash of lightning, and I saw the two tents heaving around in the wind. Then it clicked in my mind. "There are two tents!" I bawled. "We've got only one!"

I saw Coxie nodding for a split second – then something even weirder happened.

The zipper of one of the tents opened, and Dad put his head out. "Tom? Is that you? Where are you?" he yelled.

There was a tremendous crack of thunder, and then my own voice answered him from the tent.

"In the tent, of course!"

I heard Coxie give a sort of gargle of dismay and saw him pull his hands apart – and then the rain stopped, and we were standing by the camp-site in broad, dry daylight. And there was only one tent.

Coxie licked the raindrops off his lips and took a deep breath. I knew what he was going to say, so I butted in.

"We went back in time."

43

Chapter 9

DIGGING THE PAST

Of course, we tried it again. There didn't seem to be much danger, because if you pulled the medallions apart, you got shot back to where you started. I mean, when you started. It was sort of like a dead-man switch. If something happened you had to only let go – and bingo! You were home again.

"Try again," I urged Coxie. "Try twisting it further around."

You see, I'd seen how it probably worked. Mesh the grooves together and turn one click anticlockwise, and you'd get shot a year into the past. So it seemed reasonable that two clicks would send you two years back. So we tried it. We certainly went somewhere (somewhen?) because the tent disappeared, but it was impossible to know how far, because the bush looks more or less the same for years.

"I know how we can test it," I said. "That cable-logging scar has been there about seven years, so if we go back ten clicks it should disappear."

Coxie looked worried. "What if we go back to being two years old?"

"We won't, idiot," I said. "We stayed our right ages during the storm."

"Yes, but we were there twice over. And what would we have thought if we'd looked out of our tent last year and seen our this-year-selves standing in the rain?" said Coxie.

"We'd have thought we were seeing things," I said. "Like Dad did. Come on – take us back ten years."

"We shouldn't..."

"I will then." I grabbed the medallions and fitted them together, face to face. I felt the grooves lock in, and then I shut my eyes and twisted, counting clicks. I heard Coxie coughing. It sounded as if he was about to throw up. "What is it? Asthma again?" I asked.

"No," moaned Coxie, holding his belly. "I'm carsick. Sort of. I opened my eyes and saw the light flickering. Those were years going by!"

It was daylight, this time. The camp had gone, and the ground looked different. Some of the jack-jumper nests weren't there, and a fallen log had turned back into a tree. I looked up the hill to where the cable-logging scar should have been and, of course, it wasn't there. The hill was covered with thick, green bush.

"Yes!" I said. Still holding the medallions together, I started walking towards the muddy creek.

"We ought to stay put, shouldn't we?" said Coxie. "I mean – what if we end up somewhere else when you take us back?"

"Like inside a tree?" I said. "We won't, idiot. No one's ever found a tree with two boy skeletons in it around here, have they?"

"That doesn't mean there won't be one," grumbled Coxie. "Tom, this is dangerous."

"Can't see how," I said. "We can get back home in a second. Come on."

I wouldn't have recognized that creek. Instead of being muddy and silted up, it was clear and deep, like the one at our camp. I prowled upstream, looking for the place where we'd found the skull. We couldn't really pinpoint it, because there was a lot more of the creek underground now. We could hear the water gurgling away to itself down under the ferns.

"I wonder just where it is," I said.

"Where what is?"

"Well, I guess it's back underground. We haven't been here to detect it yet. In this time, we were only little kids."

"It can't be in two places at once," said Coxie. But I pointed out that *we* had been.

Then I had an idea. "Hey! We could dig up the skull now, and this time we can keep it!"

Coxie started making difficulties.

(a) We didn't have a spade.

(b) If we took the skull out now, it wouldn't be there when we came to dig it out in nine years.

"So what?" I said.

"So we'd undo the last year of our lives," said Coxie. "We won't find the skull and the medallion because they won't be there to find, your dad won't tell the police, and we won't find the second medallion, so we won't be here now."

"But we did and we are," I argued. "We'd have the medallions because we could find them now instead."

Coxie didn't agree. "You can't change things that have already happened, Tom! It isn't right."

"Look," I said. "I want to try. What harm can it do?"

Coxie stuck his chin out.

I tried to talk him around. I argued with him. I tried to persuade him. I explained it over and over. "We'd be in the same situation, only better," I said. "We'd have both medallions and the skull, too."

"If you dig out that medallion now, what happens to the ones we've got?" asked Coxie.

"How should I know? I suppose we'd have three."

"But one would be the same one twice over," said Coxie.

"So? Back at the camp-site we were there twice over," I said.

"What if you find that one and the ones we've got disappear?"

"Why should they?" I asked. "In any case, only one of them would. The other one would still be up the hill, and we could find it again if we needed to. Don't be such a worry-wart."

He stopped arguing in the end. We went back to the camp-site, and I pulled the medallions apart. Actually, I was glad to let them go – my hands were aching from keeping up the pressure. Our tent popped into sight, and I grabbed the spade I'd left leaning against a tree.

"I reckon I could get to like this time travel," I said.

I dug a couple of rubber bands out of my pocket – the heavy-duty ones the post office people put around parcels to hold them together – and handed them to Coxie. "When we get there, I'll twist these around the medallions so I don't have to keep holding onto them all the time," I said. Then I tucked the spade under my arm and slotted the medallions together.

The rubber bands worked well. Back at the creek, I was just about to start digging, when I had an even better idea. "If we go back to the creek at the time we first found it, we can pinpoint the place where we ought to dig," I said. "That'll save making too much of a mess of the banks." We tried that, but we kept arriving in the middle of the stormy night, so we gave up and tried the year before. That was better, because the bank was already starting to collapse with the run-off from the cable-logging scar. "About here," I said.

I dug about a square metre and, let me tell you, it wasn't easy. The bank was crumbling, but there were roots and rocks and a lot of cold water. I dug and dug, and we jumped back and forth a couple of years either side, but we never found the skull.

Later, I found out there was a good reason for that, but just then all I got was a lot of blisters and a really bad temper.

Our Lone Adventure lasted just two days, and I didn't do any more digging. We messed about with the medallions a bit more, but after a while, it got boring. It was really difficult to tell whether or not things had changed in the bush. We could focus on one tree and see it getting younger and older by stages, or we could see a jack-jumper nest disappear by going back a year or so, but that was all.

Further back in the past, the road changed and a lot of the rubbish disappeared, but we didn't see anything really dramatic. I'd sort of hoped for bushrangers burying gold, or Aborigines hunting kangaroos, but we saw only one other person once, and he was in the distance. We heard axes over the hill, and I wanted to go over and show ourselves to the woodcutters, and then disappear in front of them, but Coxie wouldn't agree.

The only interesting thing that happened, really, was when I found a page out of a newspaper. The date was 1942, which was when the second world war was going on, but the good old Asbestos Ranges looked just the same as ever.

"This isn't much fun," I said to Coxie. "We'll have to try it out at home. Hey! I could go to my own first birthday!"

"No, you couldn't," said Coxie. "Not unless you waited for your next birthday to do it. This goes back only in years, not months or weeks or days. It's always autumn."

"Well, how come we ended up in the middle of the night last year?" I asked. "If you're right, we should have gotten there the same time of day as we left here."

"Yeah, and we'd have walked right into our last year's camp by mistake!" said Coxie.

"That would have been fun," I said.

We never did find out exactly how the medallions chose the time of day, but I reckon they were a bit on the blink. After all, they were old.

You wouldn't think time travel could be boring, would you? But it is, if there's nothing to see but trees and bits of rubbish and creeks. Even when we went back one hundred and fifty clicks, the only thing that really happened was that the rubbish and the road and camp-site disappeared. Just for fun, I tried out the CB that time. I called Mr Watts but, of course, he didn't answer. How could he? His grandfather hadn't been born yet.

Come to think of it, I can claim to have made the earliest ever call on CB radio, years before it was even invented.

Chapter 10

HERO OF HISTORY?

It's weird, but we spent all those hours time travelling and toing and froing through the years, and Mr Watts, who was only a few hundred metres away, never missed us. We got very tired though, because the time we spent in last year or the year before that or last century didn't count in this year. If we set the medallions working at five past ten in the morning and spent two hours digging up a creek bank in the past, we'd come back to five past ten on the day we left – or thereabouts. As I said, they weren't entirely accurate.

It counted for us though, so when Mr Watts came to collect us on Wednesday afternoon, we were tired out. After all, I reckon we'd actually lived about sixty hours instead of forty-eight. Coxie looked really done in, and Mr Watts gave him a sharp look. "Not been sleeping so well, Coxie?"

Coxie managed a weak smile. "I kept thinking of jack-jumpers."

Mr Watts looked at the sky. "I reckon it's about time we hit the road – it's going to rain."

Of course, we couldn't talk about the medallions on the way home, and Coxie was dropped off first. I tried to ring him a few times, but the line was always engaged (his mum's always on the phone!), so after a bit, I gave up. I couldn't go and see him, because after we got back from the Ranges, the weather broke up and it never seemed to stop raining. I didn't experiment on my own, because Coxie had

taken the first medallion home with him. As it turned out, it was lucky he had.

While I was waiting, I drew up a list of things I wanted to do with the medallions. I'd been joking when I suggested going to my own first birthday. I knew I couldn't crash the party, because Mum and Dad wouldn't know me (how could they?), and I didn't think they'd believe me if I said I was a long-lost cousin. I could think of plenty to do, though. Like going back to the day Brett Fleming knocked me over and kicked me in the playground, and teaching him a lesson. Or revisiting the week I'd missed out on school camp because I had chickenpox. I could still nip back two years and go to camp after all. I could spend a whole year going back in my own life and righting a few private wrongs. It would be easy – just a matter of waiting for the right dates to come around.

I might even arrange to provide my younger self with the answers to that maths test I did so badly in – that cost me a trip to the footy because Dad made me stay home and study.

After that, I could get down to some serious history changing.

When we got back to school on the Monday, I hustled Coxie into the library (Mrs Wattledown was the only one in there) and showed him my list. "Look, these are some of the things I want us to do with the medallions. Not much ever happened around here, but it'd be a laugh if we ever get to Sydney. See, we could go and watch the First Fleet sail in and wait on the wharf to meet them! That'd rewrite history in a big way! Or, I could take a hammer and chisel back to the fifteenth century and cut some mysterious codes into a rock at the bluff. That'd keep the scientists guessing – we could even sign our names! They'd never pin anything on us, because the codes would be hundreds of years old. Then we could go overseas and knock off a few people that need it."

"Like who?"

"Well – like Henry the Eighth; he cut off the heads of all his wives, so why shouldn't we shoot him before he starts chopping? That way we'd save all those lives. We'd be heroes!"

"He beheaded only two of them," said Coxie. "A Catherine and an Anne. He divorced another Catherine and another Anne, the Jane died, and the third Catherine survived."

"We could kill off Hitler, too," I pointed out. "And that bloke who murdered people in America. We could be time-travelling troubleshooters – like Superman, only better."

"No, we couldn't," said Coxie. "We can't afford to go to Sydney, let alone America."

"Aha!" I said. "I've got all that worked out. We've only got to wait and watch the news, and next time someone finds some stolen money or wins the lottery, we note the date, wait a year, and go back and do it first. We'll be rich and heroes of history!"

I suppose I was carried away with my own brilliant plans, because it took me quite a few minutes to realize Coxie was looking less than thrilled.

"Come on," I told him, "it'll be really cool. Don't you see? We'll be rich and famous. We can go back through history and fix up things!"

"I don't think we should use them again," said Coxie.

"Oh, come on!" I said. "Don't be chicken!"

"I'm not," said Coxie, "but I don't want to kill people. And we can't start messing around with history. If we change the past, we'll change the present."

"Tell you what," I said, "we won't kill anyone. We'll just rescue people who are going to be killed. If we find out a kid got run over on June 2, 1978, we can wait until June the first this year, then nip back to '78 and warn him not to walk down the street. We could disguise ourselves in capes and masks..."

"He'd think we were mad," said Coxie. "It wouldn't work. I think we ought to put the medallions back and forget them."

Put them back? I couldn't believe what I was hearing.

Put the medallions back? Miss out on the best adventure in the world?

"You don't have to use them if you're scared," I said, "but you've got no right to try to stop me. Give me the one you've got, and then you can forget the whole thing."

Coxie backed away. "No," he said.

"What d'you mean, no?"

"No, I won't give it to you. I reckon you ought to give me the one you've got."

Now that's rich, isn't it? I thought. He doesn't want to use his, but he won't let me have it. Real dog-in-the-manger stuff. "Give it here," I said, and put out my hand.

Coxie slapped my hand away, then doubled back behind me and shot out the library door. "Boys? Boys!" said Mrs Wattledown. "Where are you off to? The bell's about to go."

I chased Coxie down the hall and out behind the gymnasium. He dodged behind the equipment shed and through the place where the groundsman keeps his tools. I cornered him between the cafeteria and the fence. "Give it to me!" I said.

"No," said Coxie. "Give me yours. After all, I found them both, so really, they belong to me."

"You little creep!" I said. "After all I've done for you! You wouldn't have got into the Adventurers if it hadn't been for me! You'd never have gone near the Asbestos Ranges if it hadn't been for me! Now give me that medallion!"

"No!" yelled Coxie. "I'm telling Mr Watts!" He wriggled past me and headed up the school grounds. I don't know if he really would have gone to Mr Watts, because I grabbed him by the shoulder, hauled him around, and swung a big punch right at his chin.

It snapped his head back, and he went over backwards, cracking his head against the fence. He started crying, and

I would have felt really bad if I hadn't been so angry. Then the bell went and Coxie hauled himself up. His face was all white, tears were oozing out of his eyes, and his nose was starting to run. Over my shoulder, I could hear someone yelling. "Coxie has hurt himself! Mr Watts – Mr Watts! Coxie has hit his head! He's probably got concussion!"

Mr Watts was there in no time flat. "What's wrong? What's happened? Tom, did you see him fall?"

I felt myself turning red, because Coxie was starting to wheeze and was groping for his inhaler. I knew I shouldn't have hit him. Mr Watts got the puffer and held it steady while Coxie inhaled. "Well, Tom?"

Before I could answer, Coxie got me off the hook. "Playing – chase," he wheezed. "Slipped."

"All right, Coxie. Come into the nurse's office. Go to your class, Tom. The bell has just rung." Mr Watts put his arm around Coxie's shoulder and led him away.

After that, I felt like crying, too.

Chapter 11

B.C., HERE WE COME!

That could have been the end of Coxie and me being friends, and if he'd ratted on me to Mr Watts, it would have been.

It's hard to feel proud of yourself when you've punched someone smaller and weaker, and he hasn't turned you in, so by lunch-time, I'd decided to apologize. If Coxie tried to hang a punch on me, I'd reckon we were even, and I'd get the medallion from him any way I could. But Coxie was one step ahead of me when we met in the library after the lunch bell. "Tom, there's a good reason I don't want to use those medallions again," he said.

I folded my arms like a bully. "What?"

Coxie rubbed his jaw and waggled it back and forth, and I remembered I'd meant to apologize. "Sorry," I said.

"Those medallions," said Coxie. "We found them with bones, didn't we?"

"So what?"

"So," said Coxie, "what do you reckon happened to the real owners?"

"They died ages ago, I suppose," I said. "If it was their bones we found."

"Right," said Coxie. "They must have gone back or forwards in time once too often."

"Maybe they died of old age..." Then I blinked. I mean, I felt myself blink, as I realized what he'd said. "Forwards in time?"

Coxie shrugged. "I suppose you can go forwards."

"Let's!"

Coxie groaned. "No. No. No. Tom, haven't you heard a word I've been saying?"

"Of course I have, idiot. I want to try forwards. Just think – we could see ourselves at eighteen! See what sort of car we get to drive!"

"Better go back if we must go anywhere," said Coxie.

"We've already been back," I said.

"Back to the time the medallions got buried," said Coxie. "I want to find out what happened. I want to know where they came from."

So did I. And, of course, that meant we had to go back to the Asbestos Ranges. And that wasn't as simple as you might think.

Dad was too busy to take us, and Mum's car can't make it up the hill. Mr Watts said we couldn't have another Lone Adventure, because it wasn't our turn.

"So what do we do?" I asked.

Coxie shrugged. "My mum'll take us. I told her about those ferns we saw along the creek – she wants to sketch them for the botany club."

"Great," I said.

Coxie's mum made as many preparations for a half-day picnic as my mum would have made for a week, but in the end, we got away. She didn't like the road into the Asbestos Ranges very much, but Coxie kept saying it got better further on. It never did, of course, but by the time Mrs Cox realized that, we were there. We ate our picnic, then Coxie said we wanted to climb up the hill.

"I don't think you'd better go all the way up there, dear," said Mrs Cox. "You'll tire yourselves."

Of course, that didn't stop us. We just stepped behind a big tree and clicked ourselves back a couple of years. I snapped the rubber bands around the medallions.

I was still annoyed with Coxie, so I tried being sarcastic. "OK, brain," I said. "How are you going to do this? Since we can visit only one day a year, we might have to spend a whole 365 days trying to catch up with them, and that's just not on. Your mum wouldn't bring us back tomorrow, even, let alone every day for a year."

"We can try," said Coxie. "With luck they stayed around a while. I reckon we ought to go up to the top of the hill, then we'll have a good view all around. We can check the whole area in each year, and if we see any sign of a camp or a house, we can get a better idea of when we need to try again."

"Oh, sure," I said. "You're going to click these things back 5,500 times? Your hands will drop off."

"No, they won't," said Coxie patiently. "There are a hundred notches, so if you twist the medallions right around once, you've got a century. That means I have to make about 52 complete twists, and then start narrowing it down."

He was right, and that annoyed me more. We climbed to the top of the hill, and stood in the bare place where the cable-loggers had stripped away the trees and undergrowth. It was an uncomfortable place to stand, because the rocks were sticking out and loose soil kept getting in our shoes. "OK," I said. I couldn't help feeling a bit excited, even though it wasn't what I'd wanted to do. "We've got a good view, so let's go. B.C., here we come!"

Coxie took us back a few more years to where the trees hadn't been taken. Then he made one whole revolution with the medallions, and we had our first (and last) look at 1880. We also had our first – and last – look at a Tasmanian tiger, or *thylacine*. These animals have been extinct since 1936.

"I wish I'd brought Dad's camera," I said.

Since then, I've thought about how we should have caught it and a few of its mates, and brought them back to the 1990s and let them go. That way, they wouldn't be extinct anymore. I wish we had done it, but it's too late now.

Coxie revolved the medallions, and we saw 1780. "How weird," I said. "The First Fleet hasn't happened yet! It'll be another eight years before Captain Phillip sails into Sydney Harbour."

Coxie shivered. He still wasn't saying much.

1680.

1580.

1480.

1380.

"We're back in the Middle Ages!" I said. "They're all dying of the Black Death over in Europe."

I felt my knees start to shake. If I'd done what I'd planned and gone over to Europe to kill off a few villains before they got villainous, I might have died of the plague myself. I suppose they could cure the Black Death today, but how would we ever convince the doctor that that was what I had? At least here in Tasmania, the Black Death never happened. There are some compensations for being isolated from the rest of the world.

In a few minutes, we were back before the time of Christ. "Don't lose count," I said. "We've got to go back 5,200 years, and that puts us in – in..."

"About 3000 B.C.," said Coxie shortly.

By now, the trees were different, and the air didn't smell the same. Coxie stopped making complete sweeps around the medallions and started clicking back year by year. It took quite a long time, because we had to stop at every click and scan around to see if we could see anyone. Sometimes it was night, sometimes it was morning.

Sometimes we landed in a storm, or a heat wave. I looked up at the sky. No factory smoke on the horizon, not a jet trail in sight...

"We're about the right year now," said Coxie. "Keep your eyes peeled down there."

I guess it was because we were both staring down the hillside at the creek that it was such a shock when someone spoke behind us.

Chapter 12

LIZBA

I don't know what she said, because I was too shocked to be hearing a voice at all in that place. Besides Coxie's, I mean. Anyway, I snapped around so fast I nearly fell over.

She was lying on the hill just behind us, and she looked really sick. Her face was pale and sweaty, and her mouth looked sort of blue. The pupils of her eyes were so wide you could hardly tell what colour the irises were.

She was wearing a sort of wet suit – well, that was what it looked like. Or maybe it was more like overalls. It was the sort of thing you might see people wearing in a chemistry lab or a science fiction movie.

I think she was surprised to see us, too. I know she wasn't very pleased.

"I need my pack," she said. Her voice sounded funny, as if the accent was wrong, but I understood her all right. She waved her hand behind her, and I saw what she wanted, a sort of black case on the ground.

She was obviously hurt, so I went over to get it for her and handed it over. Then I backed off, just in case she did have the plague.

"Who are you?" I asked, but she didn't seem to hear. She didn't seem to be able to open the case, either, so Coxie and I had to move back to help her. I don't know how it actually worked, because it just came open in our hands.

The stuff inside was weird-looking, too, so we just had to keep on picking things out and holding them up until we

came to the ones she wanted. I think one of them was some sort of anesthetic or stimulant or something. It was in a syringe, and she injected it right through her clothes into her leg.

It started working quite quickly and, within a couple of minutes, her eyes changed. The pupils shrank back to normal, and I could see her eyes were brown, like my mum's. She still looked odd. It wasn't so much her clothes as her face. Lizba looked old-fashioned and foreign, high-tech and familiar, all at the same time. Yeah, her face was from another time.

The medication made Lizba feel a lot better, I think, because she was able to tell us about the other thing she wanted out of her kit. It was a sort of gauge (she called it a diagnostic) that you could run over your body to tell what was wrong with you. Whatever it told the woman was bad news, I could see. Her face went sort of slack, and then she made an "oh, well!" sort of face.

"So endeth the lesson," she said, which seemed a weird thing to be saying in 3570 B.C.

"Who are you?" I asked again. "Why aren't you pleased to see us? We can help you..."

She looked up at us. "The fact that you are here may mean that I have failed. You should not be here, although I do thank you for allowing me to treat my injury."

"You shouldn't be here, either," I said, "since you're not an Aborigine."

Coxie and I sat down on the ground. "Are these yours?" asked Coxie. He held up the medallions, and she made a face.

"When did you find them?"

"We found one last year, and the other a month or so back," I said. Then I realized what I was saying, and gave her the dates instead.

"The 20th century," murmured the woman. "If only I had had time to plan! I might have known they'd fall into the wrong hands! I did know... Oh, why wouldn't he listen?"

"What's going on?" I asked. "We still don't know who you are – although I expect you're the skull..." I was about to say "skull we found", but I caught myself in time.

She knew what I meant, though, because she gave a sort of grim smile and said, "You found my skull, did you? I hope it didn't give you too much of a shock. I understand people of the 20th century had an unhealthy fear of bodily remains."

"Oh no, I thought it was cool," I said. "I wanted it for my mum to put in her cabinet."

The woman sighed. "How strange – " She closed her eyes for a moment, then opened them again. "You must go – but wait – I wonder what would be best?"

"Who are you?" said Coxie. "When are you from?"

"I am Lizba Smith, and I was born in 3152 A.D. I live – will be living in Greater Launceston, in the sector of Tasmania."

"We thought you came from the past, not the future," I said, and we told her more or less what I've been telling you. She kept asking questions, about where we had found the medallions and the bones, and what, precisely, had we done with them since.

"I had hoped this would not happen," she said. "I thought I had rid history of those cursed things. But now, since you have found them, we must decide what to do." I liked the way she said that, as if she thought we were old enough to be sensible. "It's just as well you are the only two who know about them," she said. "The fewer who know of their existence and purpose, the better."

"Where did you get them?" asked Coxie. "And what happened to you?"

Lizba told us that she and her lab partner, Palmer, had been involved in what she called "temporal research" for years. That meant they had been learning all they could about time.

They were meant to keep it as pure research, but one day they came up with a formula that seemed so interesting that Palmer persuaded Lizba to try it out in practical application. They went back to the laboratory one night after hours, and Lizba made a time medallion.

"Palmer insisted on testing the medallion," explained Lizba. "I had grave doubts, because I knew it needed many more months of work for safety, and besides, there were the ethical questions to be hammered out.

"Scientific research carries enormous responsibilities. There are two questions we scientists must always ask: 'Can we?' and 'Should we?' Although I had worked with Palmer for many years, I wasn't sure that he could be trusted to consider the second question. I also felt there was some kind of flaw in our research, and for some time, I managed to stall Palmer while I tried to work out just what it was.

"I thought I had talked Palmer out of making any rash moves, but then we heard that our funding had been cut and our work was to be wound down. Palmer was very angry – far more so than I would have expected." She frowned. "I should tell you something about Palmer and about the society in which we live.

"Our time is one of social and economic upheaval. The government is split on an issue which directly affects all of us – and especially our children.

"It has been suggested that society would benefit if all luxuries were removed from our lives." She smiled slightly. "None of us likes the idea of giving up our favourite indulgences, but I feel sure we would comply if it were not for one thing – pets.

"Pets are deemed a luxury," said Lizba. "One party favours the complete – painless – destruction of all non-useful livestock, while the other feels pets are essential to the emotional well-being of society."

Coxie looked green about the gills, and I knew he was thinking of his cockatoo, Cracker. Coxie thinks an awful lot of that bird.

"Both sides believe they are acting in the best interests of our country," said Lizba, "and each has a valid point of view. There is a referendum approaching. One party will vote one way, and the other another. One man, a political independent named Kane, has the casting vote.

"Palmer and I suspect Kane will vote for the second option." Lizba sighed. "I have always known that Palmer

supported the first option, but I truly believed he would not allow his political opinions to affect his work. I was wrong."

"What happened?" I asked.

Lizba shrugged. "He was spending more time with his less-reputable political cronies and less at the lab, while I went over and over our computer notes, trying to identify the flaw. And then – I found it. And I knew that if Palmer tested the medallion as it was, he would be killed."

We gaped at her, then Coxie gave me an I-told-you-so look. "But it didn't kill us," I said.

"Then you were very lucky. I realized that, in making one medallion, we had neglected to balance the forces. Time runs both forwards and back, so there must be two balanced forces to make time travel safe. That was the flaw. To travel safely, we needed two medallions and two or more travellers.

"I added my findings to our notes, and that night, I made the second, complementary medallion. Since I knew Palmer would insist on the test, and I had no wish for anyone else to use the formula, I then changed my mind and decided to destroy the records."

"Did you?" asked Coxie.

I could see he felt as sick as I did. We really could have killed ourselves. I remembered how I had messed about with the one medallion, making the numbers light up, shoving my fingernail into the grooves. If I'd set it off accidentally, I could have ended up stranded anywhen – or dead.

"I was about to wipe the computer's memory when Palmer came back to the lab," said Lizba. "He was in a state of high excitement, and he *persuaded* me to co-operate with his plans for immediate departure."

She sighed.

"Palmer was always ambitious. I thought at first he simply wanted to run the test, and then announce our great discovery in a bid to obtain more funding, but it was more than that. He told me he wanted to change recent history. I tried to reason with him, but he was beyond reason. He was determined to force me to set the medallion to take us back forty years."

"What for?" asked Coxie.

"Oh dear," said Lizba. "This is difficult to explain. He wished to force Kane to compromise his vote in the referendum."

"How could going back forty years do that?" I asked. "Was he going to kill this Kane off as a kid?" It sounded a lot like the plans I'd had.

"Not quite," said Lizba. "He told me he intended to kidnap the child Kane and bring him forwards to our time to use as a hostage.

"With the threat of not only instant death for his adult self if the child was killed, but also of instant erasure of all his life's work, Palmer was sure Kane would fall in with his wishes."

"How did you get here, though?" I asked. "Now, I mean? This isn't where Palmer wanted to be."

"I programmed the medallions to bring us to an earlier date in time, much further back than Palmer wanted to come," said Lizba, with a shrug. "He thinks I have brought him to the time he wanted. He's gone off to search out the child Kane."

She made a face. "As you can see, he made sure I wouldn't run away." She eased herself over a bit on the ground, and I noticed she was using her hands, not her legs.

"Are you OK?" I asked. "Has that injection made your legs go to sleep?"

Lizba didn't answer. The grey look was coming back into her face.

"We'd better get you some proper help," I said. "Get you to a doctor or something."

"She needs a drink, too," said Coxie.

Lizba shook her head. "No need," she said. "I shall do well enough now." I noticed she was starting to wheeze a bit, the way Coxie does when he's getting an asthma attack.

"What can we do to help you?" I asked. "Can we take you back to your own time? Can they fix you up there?"

"Certainly they can," said Lizba, "but I cannot take the risk. It is better if I die."

Chapter 13

PALMER

She said it the way you might say "I'm going shopping," and it took a few seconds for her meaning to sink in.

"What do you mean, better?" I said. "If you get yourself fixed up, you'll be able to come back and stop Palmer."

"No," said Lizba. She stuck her chin out and looked stubborn. She was every bit as pigheaded as Coxie. "I came back to this time to be sure no one would ever be able to misuse the medallions," she said. "Not Palmer, not anyone. I must stick to that decision."

"You could warn this Kane man," I said. "You could go back and have his parents hide him away from the time he's born. Or you could pull the same thing on Palmer that he's trying to pull on Kane. Kidnap his younger self."

"Wrong is wrong, for me as much as for Palmer," said Lizba. "And who is to be the judge and executioner? The most I can do is prevent Palmer from distorting history and using my work for his own ends. I know he's wrong, but one person's good is another's evil, and he was responsible for much of the original research..."

"Quite right," said a voice.

I suppose we should have been wondering when this Palmer person would turn up, but we'd been too caught up in Lizba's story to ask. And now, here he was.

I reckon Palmer was younger than Lizba, and he had the same out-of-time look about him. He was tall and dark-haired, and he looked like a reasonable person – until you

74

saw his eyes. They were dark and round like a cockatoo's. He was holding a nasty-looking little gadget in one hand. It didn't look much like any weapon I've ever seen, but you could tell what it was from the look on his face and the way he was pointing it at us. I knew it must be the one he'd used to force Lizba to bring him here.

"Still with us, Lizba?" asked Palmer.

"As you see," said Lizba.

"I'm glad to see it. I was afraid you'd die before I was finished with you. Who are your friends?"

"They have nothing to do with this."

"I think you've been lying to me, Lizba," said Palmer. "I think you made more medallions. Otherwise, how did these children get here? Somehow I don't believe they'll be of much help to you." And he sneered at Coxie and me.

I don't like people pointing weapons at me, and I don't like being sneered at, either. I'd love to have given Palmer one on the nose, but you don't go around hitting adults. Not if you know what's good for you.

"You brought me to the wrong time, didn't you, Lizba?" said Palmer. "This is no more 3160 A.D. than I'm the Pied Piper. Now take me to the right time."

"Take yourself, Palmer," said Lizba weakly. "I am dying, and I want to do it without having to look at you."

Palmer clicked his tongue and retrieved two medallions from his pocket. I could see that they were exactly the same as the ones we had, except that there was a sort of clip that held them together instead of my rubber band. In fact, they were the ones we had, but a few thousand years younger. "You want me to use these and take myself to 3160, Lizba?"

Lizba nodded. "Yes."

"After all your fine words and protests, you will simply let me go on my way to do what you know I intend to do?"

"It doesn't matter anymore," said Lizba. "I am dying and will soon be out of the game. How can it matter to me anymore?" She turned her head away and began fumbling in her kit. "I have the blueprints here."

"You want me to go alone to find little Kane?" said Palmer again.

"Yes."

Palmer pushed past Coxie and me and bent over Lizba. I thought for a moment he was going to help her up, but instead he just glared. "So you'd murder me, would you, Lizba? You know better than anyone that it's death to travel alone," he said coldly. "It looks like you'll have to come with me one last time. After that, I'll have young Kane as insurance, and I'll get rid of you." He swung

around to Coxie and me. "Stand aside, you. But first, give me those medallions."

He held out his left hand, clicking his fingers impatiently. "Stop stalling. I know you must have some."

Coxie and I backed away. Neither of us wanted to be stranded in the 30th century B.C., and we didn't trust Palmer any more than Lizba did. Coxie was fumbling with the medallions, trying to get the rubber band off so he could snap us back to our own time.

Then Palmer fired the weapon.

It hit me in the chest, and for a second, I couldn't move for shock. Then I couldn't move at all. I felt myself falling, and heard the bark and leaves crunch as my body hit the ground; but I didn't feel a thing. I was cold and numb from

my neck down. It was like being turned into a statue.

After that, time seemed to stretch out, and everything seemed to be in slow motion. I know Coxie screamed, and I remember seeing Lizba bring her hand out of her pack. She was holding a weapon like Palmer's, and she pointed it directly at him. "Stand back!" she said. "I'm not coming with you. I'll kill you first."

Palmer's face turned a funny colour. He was obviously the kind of creep who can dish it out, but who can't take it. I would have told him that, but my tongue wouldn't work.

"Stand back, Palmer," said Lizba. "I'm warning you."

Palmer seemed to give up. "All right, Lizba. All right. We'll play it your way," he said casually. "You might die on the way, anyway, and where would that leave me?"

"We need to work this out," said Lizba.

"So we do. I'll just get this boy more comfortable..." Palmer came towards me. I would have spat in his eye, but I still couldn't move.

I wondered why Coxie wasn't coming to help me; then I heard him wheezing and knew he was having another attack. He was fumbling about in his day pack for his puffer.

"Leave that, you idiot!" I wanted to say. "Get the bands off the medallions and get us home!" I tried, but nothing came out but a croak.

"Let me help you," said Palmer. He put his arm around Coxie's shoulder, and his other hand came up and flipped back the clip on his set of medallions. Then he twisted the medallions.

Coxie must have noticed what he was doing a split second after I did, because I saw his eyes bulge with horror. His hands went all slack, and I heard a shuffling sort of thud as something bounced onto the ground. Then Lizba fired her weapon. It hit Palmer in the chest.

I saw Palmer start to crumple forwards. I saw Coxie buckle under his weight, but I never saw them hit the ground.

They were falling, and then they were gone.

Chapter 14

DANGER IN 3160 A.D.

My throat picked that minute to unlock, and I screamed as loudly as Coxie had.

Lizba's face was bluer than ever, and she was gulping for breath, but I think her hands were still steady as she put away the weapon.

"I'm sorry," she said.

My tongue was tingling as if I'd stuck it in hot chocolate, but my voice came back with a rush. "What do you mean, you're sorry? Where have they gone? Where's Coxie?"

"I don't know," said Lizba.

"Palmer's taken him forwards to your time, hasn't he?"

"He was too – quick for me," said Lizba. "He must have known – he needed a living companion. My fault. I planned the medallions that way – as a safety measure against being stranded – out of time. My – mistake. Never thought he'd – take the – child." She closed her eyes.

Don't die, I thought in a panic. That'll leave me here all alone!

I don't think it had really hit me then – that Coxie was gone, and that I'd probably starve to death out here in the Ranges, more than 49 centuries before I'd even be born. There wasn't a lot to eat in this part of the world in 3000 B.C., even if I could have gotten to it. And I couldn't.

I was paralyzed even worse than Lizba.

Then Lizba spoke to me again. "Can you – move – at all?"

I tried to lift my hand. "No." I felt as if I'd never move again. Like stone.

"I think – your friend – dropped something. Over – there."

I swivelled my eyes to where she was looking, to the place where Coxie and Palmer had been. There was Coxie's puffer on the ground, and beside it, a gleam of silver.

"He left our medallions!" I said.

"We can – follow them," said Lizba.

"I can't reach the medallions," I agonized.

I could feel a tingling now in my shoulders. It was like an itch I couldn't scratch. After a few minutes, it spread down my arms, and soon my hands were burning and throbbing. It really hurt, like it does when you're silly enough to try and thaw frozen fingers under the hot tap. My fingers felt too big, as if they'd split their skins any minute, like bursting sausages. I groaned, feeling the sweat come out on my face like it had on Lizba's. I hurt like mad.

"Can you – reach – medallions?" asked Lizba.

"No," I said. "I told you, I can't move."

Actually, I could move my hands now, but it hurt terribly.

"Try!" gasped Lizba. "Your circulation is – coming back – that's why it hurts. You can move and you – must. Get those medallions and – bring them to me."

"You get them," I said.

Lizba shook her head. "Palmer – wasn't as gentle – on me as – on you. My back is – broken."

"You'll have to get to a doctor!" I said.

"First – need – medallions."

After that, of course, it was up to me. It took me longer than I care to remember to crawl those few metres to the medallions and the puffer and get them to Lizba. I think she knew how hard it was, because she kept on encouraging me the whole time.

"Good work. Now, take us forwards."

She helped me get the setting right. It wasn't really necessary to frog-hop forwards by centuries the way Coxie and I had done. There was a way you could set the exact year you wanted. We weren't sure what year Palmer had set, or if he'd set it properly, but Lizba had a good idea that he'd be trying to carry out his original plan.

When we reached 3160, I saw that the Asbestos Ranges had changed a lot more in the twelve centuries between our time and Lizba's, than they had in the 30 centuries before. The trees were gone, and the hills were bare and rocky. Nearly all the soil had been washed away.

"This is where – lab will – be in – ten years," gasped Lizba. "Kane – grew up – some distance – away."

I didn't care about Kane. I just wanted to find Coxie, and I didn't have to look far. Just down the hill a way, I saw Coxie and Palmer. Palmer was stretched out on the ground like I'd been, but it was easy to see that he wasn't going to live long.

He had "landed" on a tough bit of rock. His leg was severely broken and twisted up behind him. I could see the blood trickling slowly from a massive head wound. Coxie was just next to Palmer, flat on his face.

Fortunately, Coxie looked a lot better, except he was gasping like crazy. Palmer must have broken his fall. I hauled myself down to Coxie and gave him his puffer. I had to help him use it; then I left him to get his breath. My legs were burning now, although my feet were still stony, and I could move a lot better than I had.

After I'd helped Coxie, I looked back on Palmer. He was lucid and looking at me. I'll never forget that look. He knew he was dying, and he knew he couldn't do a single thing about it without our help.

"Tom, the medallions!" It was hardly any more than a breath, but I heard Lizba calling and understood. By now, she was in a bad way. Palmer was lying down, swearing blue murder as he regained his senses.

I didn't want to move Lizba; I knew you shouldn't move people with broken bones. But Lizba said she'd be OK. I walked up to Palmer and took the medallions out of his hands. He was powerless to stop me. I remember the light dying out of his cockatoo eyes as he realized that he was about to die. We did not intend to help him.

"Come on, Coxie. Help me carry Lizba."

Coxie stumbled weakly over to us.

I thought that would be the end of it with Palmer dead, but Lizba had something else she needed done. "Tom, you'll have to – end it," she said. Her voice was nearly down to a whisper by now, and for a moment, I had the gruesome feeling she was asking me to shoot her. But she wasn't. I should have known Lizba wouldn't leave any loose ends. Even though she was in what doctors call a critical condition, her brain still worked better than mine. And maybe, I thought, if we did what she wanted, she'd let us get her to a doctor.

Chapter 15

THE END

What Lizba needed me to do was destroy the notes she'd left in her computer. She'd meant to do it herself, remember, but Palmer had gotten to her first.

Lizba described exactly what she needed me to do, and how I was to do it. "There won't – be much – time," she said. "By now – it's day after – we left. Medallions' setting – been – changed."

What she meant was, the medallions would snap you back to the instant you left only if you didn't change the settings in between.

"There may – be – people in – lab... people – like – Palmer. You must – act – fast. I won't – be able – help you. You – you could – be – killed." I could scarcely hear the last word.

Coxie didn't want me to do it. He was all for taking Lizba forwards to her time, then going straight back home. "We shouldn't change anything else!" he yelled at me. He was still a bit wheezy.

"This isn't changing the past," I pointed out. "Come on, Coxie – you're wasting time! It's fixing up the future."

Coxie stuck his jaw out at me and shook his head. "We've done enough."

"No," I argued. "We're putting it back the way it should have been."

"Please," whispered Lizba.

"Do what you like, then," said Coxie. "I'm not coming."

"You can take me home first," he continued.

So that's what we did. Lizba set the medallions for our own time, and we were back on the hill, with Lizba lying on the bare ground where the cable-logging had left the rocks and stubble. "Even in – your time – the destruction?" she said.

"People have to have jobs," I said. "They're growing plantation trees, but sometimes they still cut the old growth forests. They can't seem to wait for the plantations to grow."

"Always – the hard – decisions," said Lizba. "Have you made – your decision, – Tom? I – cannot – promise – safety."

"I'll come with you to the future on one condition, that you must let us get you to a doctor," I said, although, now that I was home, I quite definitely didn't want to go time travelling again. Not with someone who might die at any minute. "Are you coming with us, Coxie?"

Coxie shook his head.

"We owe it to Lizba," I said. "She won't try to help herself if we don't."

"Maybe, but I owe it to my mum to stay alive. She's already lost Dad and Michael."

He had a point. He wasn't about to trade the present for the future. As far as I could see, we had to fix the future to keep the present safe from other people like Palmer, but I didn't have time to try to talk Coxie into it. "See you, then," I said.

Lizba was too far gone to set the medallions, so I did it, using the pair that looked newer because they had the clip. I stood close to Lizba, set the numbers and twisted.

I heard Coxie start to say something, the light flickered – and I was standing in a corridor. The floor and ceiling were crawling with pulsing light. "Where are we?" I

whispered. I had to crouch to hear Lizba's reply.

"Go through that hatch – quickly. Take this. It is set for electronic equipment."

I took the weapon she handed me and went through the nearest door. There was the lab room, just as Lizba had described. There was the computer, just as she'd described. The room was empty, but as I started towards the computer, I heard voices through the next door.

"Seal the doors while I search – from what Palmer says, Lizba may attempt to destroy... Who's there?"

I don't know how they heard me. Maybe I gasped, or maybe they heard my heartbeats. They certainly sounded loud enough to me. I shot back out to Lizba. "There are people in there!" I hissed. "They know Palmer!"

"Warned – you," whispered Lizba. "Hurry, Tom..."

I knew I had to do it now or never. If I waited any longer, the doors would be sealed.

I was just in time. By now, three or four scientists in white uniforms like Lizba's had come in. They were holding weapons like the one I had, and they were clustered around the computer. One was punching the keyboard. I don't know if they were looking for Lizba's notes or sealing the door, but I didn't give them a chance to finish.

I crept up behind them. I couldn't get by, so I got down on my knees and took aim. I steadied the weapon against my other arm and fired.

The computer melted like cheese under a grill, and the scientists jumped as if I'd shot them. I bet I broke the land-speed record, making for the door. As I went, I pried off the clips on the medallions, dived down on the floor next to Lizba, and let go.

And then we were lying on the rough, rocky side of the hill, with Coxie staring at us like an idiot. "Wait, I'll come," he was saying.

I let out my breath in a whoosh. "Too late," I said. "We did it."

So there we were, Coxie and Lizba and I, up on the hill. "Now you're – home," said Lizba. Her breathing was worse.

"We've got to get you to a hospital," I said. "How odd, we won't be finding your skull, now. I mean, we won't have found it, because you're not going to die in the past. Coxie, your mum's just down there. Give her a yell, and she can come up and help us get Lizba down to the car. Or would it be better to call an ambulance?"

"Wait," said Lizba. Her voice sounded stronger. "It will be better – to dispose of medallions – first. Shoot – the medallions – Tom. These – first... " Her hand moved to touch the pair we'd found.

I hated to do it, but time was running out for her, so I turned the weapon on the medallions. I tried to fire the weapon, but nothing happened.

"You have to activate – press – the safety." I found a little safety button on the underside and released it. The weapon seemed to illuminate. I aimed at the medallions and melted them as I'd melted the computer.

"Thank – you," said Lizba.

"These now?" I asked, pointing to the newer ones she was holding.

"No. Stand – aside – boys. And – thank you."

"What?" I said. "Hey, give those to me... "

I was too late, of course. Lizba fitted the medallions face to face and twisted...

For an instant more, we saw her lying there. I thought she smiled, and then she was gone. In the same instant, we saw something go flying out over the rocks and dirt. There was a sort of flash, and a sound you couldn't really hear.

Implosion, I think it's called.

For a moment, we stood there staring, then Coxie went over and picked up the thing that we had seen falling.

It was the medallions. Well, I think it was. It was difficult to tell, because it had corroded up into a lump of twisted metal like a burned-out plug, just like the two I'd melted.

"Travelling on just one kills you," said Coxie, aghast.

So did travelling alone. Lizba had made quite sure...

I dropped what was left of the medallions into my pocket. Then I looked at the weapon, still clutched in my hand. I couldn't throw it away, so I clicked on the safety button and shoved it in my pocket as well. Then we went back down the hill. I don't know about Coxie, but I felt as if I'd been away for weeks.

As I said before, Lizba had a lot of guts.

Chapter 16

QUESTIONS

Coxie's mum was a bit surprised to see us coming down the hill. Well, what I mean is, she was very surprised. See, she'd only just seen us step behind a tree. We had to do some fast talking to get ourselves out of that one, and the last thing I felt like doing just then was fast talking. I had too much to think about.

How would you feel if you'd just seen a person you admired shoot another person and then commit suicide?

Violence is wrong, but Lizba shot Palmer so Palmer wouldn't kidnap a child and blackmail people and deny our country all the luxuries we had worked so hard to have. Even if Lizba had destroyed the medallions in her own future, Palmer still knew almost enough to make some more.

So maybe Lizba was right to shoot Palmer. I suppose it was his own fault that we didn't try to help him in the end. He was destroyed by selfishness.

I just don't know.

You see, I can't blame Palmer entirely. He wanted to do what *he* thought was right and, in some ways, I agreed with him. Sometimes you can't have luxuries like pets and treats if other people have to suffer because of it.

But Coxie would suffer without his cockatoo, I'm sure. And I really didn't like the way Palmer went about it all; he wanted to force everyone else to do what he wanted. He'd do anything to get his way, and he thought the end justified the means. As I said, there was a lot to think about. They were both dangerous people, but I know who I'd rather have as a friend.

Would you believe that during the whole adventure Coxie's mum was the only person who ever noticed anything strange? When I consider all the things that could have gone wrong, it makes me go cold.

That day out at the Ranges with Coxie's mum was almost the end of the whole adventure. I still have the twisted remains of the medallions, but there's no way you can tell what they were, and certainly no way they will ever work again.

I asked Coxie if he wanted to go back to the creek. Coxie just wants to forget the whole thing. He doesn't even go to Adventurers much any more – he reckons he's had enough adventures.

Oh – there is still one odd thing – the skull. I'd really like to know what happened to that. Is it still in the bottom left-hand drawer of someone's filing cabinet, or did it vanish when Lizba destroyed the medallions and herself? I suppose it all depends on which way Lizba went.

If she sent herself back into the past, there's every chance that her skull is still in that filing cabinet, and that it contains the proof that our whole adventure really happened.

But I suppose I'll never know.

Coxie won't discuss it, so one day I might ask Dad if he remembers the opalized skull. I hope he does. I don't want Lizba never to have existed, but I don't want her skull to stay in a filing cabinet, either. It isn't dignified, so one day when I'm older, I'll see what I can do.

Of course, I still have the weapon – tucked away in a shoebox under my bed. The thing is – it isn't proof of anything. It just looks like a plastic toy and it doesn't light up anymore when I push the safety button. I reckon it couldn't work – the power pack must have run down by now.

So now you know why I've gone to the trouble of writing this all out. Just so there'll be a record of a fantastic adventure that maybe never happened. But maybe it did.

GLOSSARY

Aborigine – the indigenous people of Australia

bandicoot – a small marsupial that eats insects and plants

bloke – a guy

bush – indigenous Australian forest

bushranger – a 19th-century outlaw

cockatoo – a white parrot-like bird with distinctive round eyes

collect – to pick up

conglomerate – composite rock

croc – a crocodile

cuff – to brush someone with the back of your hand

dead-man switch – a switch that needs constant, conscious pressure to work

dog-in-the-manger – a person who keeps another from enjoying something, but does not make use of it himself (See *Aesop's Fables*)

engaged – busy

First Fleet – the term for the first ships, guided by Captain Phillip, that sailed into Sydney Harbour in 1788, marking the beginning of a European presence in Australia

footy – a football game (of the game Australian Rules)

frog-hop – leap-frog

greasy – slippery and muddy

guy-rope – a rope used to secure a tent to the ground for stability

have my guts for garters – literally: to dismember; figuratively: to get in big trouble; equivalent: going to kill me

huntsman spider – a hairy, palm-sized spider commonly found in the Australian bush and, sometimes, in houses

jack-jumper – a large black ant which builds tall nests that look like volcanoes

kip – a nap

mad – crazy

mate – a friend

Piltdown Man – an elaborate hoax in England, in which the supposed skeleton of an early man was discovered. Ultimately, the find was discredited.

puffer – an inhaler that is used to relieve asthma

pull the other one – literally: pull the other leg; figuratively: I don't believe you; equivalent: you're pulling my leg

reckon – to think

rubbish – garbage

siren – a school bell

Tasmanian tiger (thylacine) – a dog-like, carnivorous marsupial, now considered extinct

tearing a strip off – literally: whipping; figuratively: getting really mad; equivalent: going to beat me to a pulp

telly – a television

thick – stupid

TITLES IN THE SERIES